When Stories Fell Like Shooting Stars

When Stories
Fell Like
Shooting Stars

by **VALISKA GREGORY**

illustrated by **STEFANO VITALE**

SIMON & SCHUSTER BOOKS FOR YOUNG READERS

SIMON & SCHUSTER BOOKS FOR YOUNG READERS
An imprint of Simon & Schuster Children's Publishing Division
1230 Avenue of the Americas, New York, New York 10020
Text copyright © 1996 by Valiska Gregory
Illustrations copyright © 1996 by Stefano Vitale
SIMON & SCHUSTER BOOKS FOR YOUNG READERS
is a trademark of Simon & Schuster.
Book design by Lucille Chomowicz
The text for this book is set in Hiroshige medium
The illustrations are rendered in oil paints on wooden boards
Printed and bound in the United States of America
First Edition
10 9 8 7 6 5 4 3 2 1
Library of Congress Cataloging-in-Publication Data
Gregory, Valiska.
When stories fell like shooting stars / by Valiska Gregory:
illustrated by Stefano Vitale.
p. cm.
Summary: When Fox sees the sun fall from the sky,
his selfish actions set in motion a series of events that lead to war,
but when Bear finds the fallen moon,
he gets the other animals to work together to return
the moon to where it belongs.
ISBN 0-689-80012-6
[1. Animals—Fiction. 2. Greed—Fiction.
3. Cooperativeness—Fiction.] I. Vitale, Stefano, ill. II. Title.
PZ7.G8624Wh 1996 95-14887
[E]—dc20

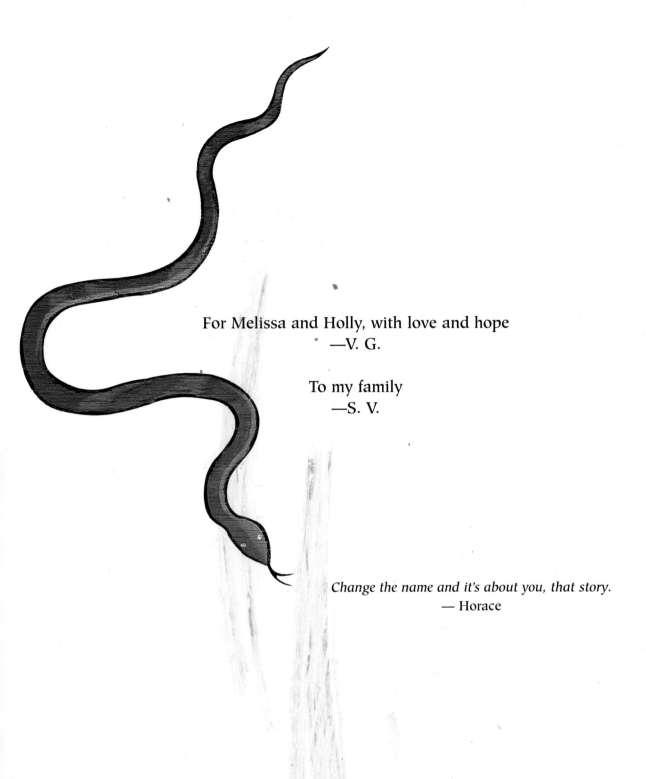

For Melissa and Holly, with love and hope
—V. G.

To my family
—S. V.

Change the name and it's about you, that story.
— Horace

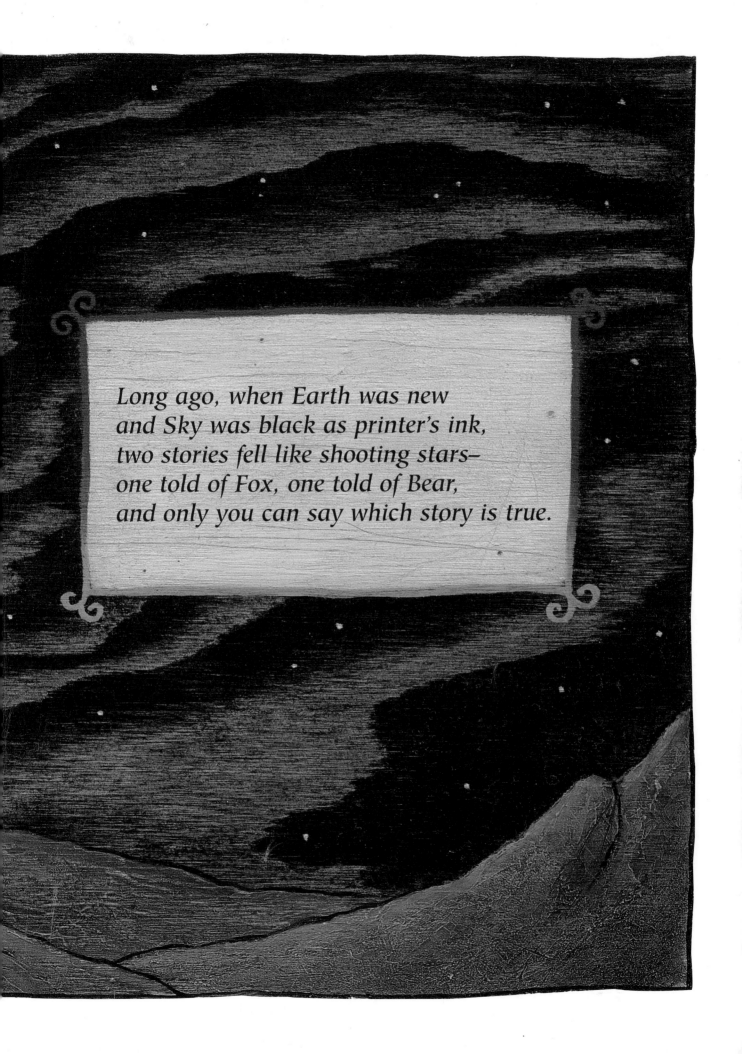

Long ago, when Earth was new
and Sky was black as printer's ink,
two stories fell like shooting stars—
one told of Fox, one told of Bear,
and only you can say which story is true.

Fox's Story

One day when Fox looked up, he saw the sun tumble from its cradle of clouds and fall like a bird into the tangled branches of a tree. It hung, a glittering coin, caught in a many-fingered net.

"This cannot be," said Fox, squinting his eyes, but there Sun was, as red as hearts and yellow as gold, trembling.

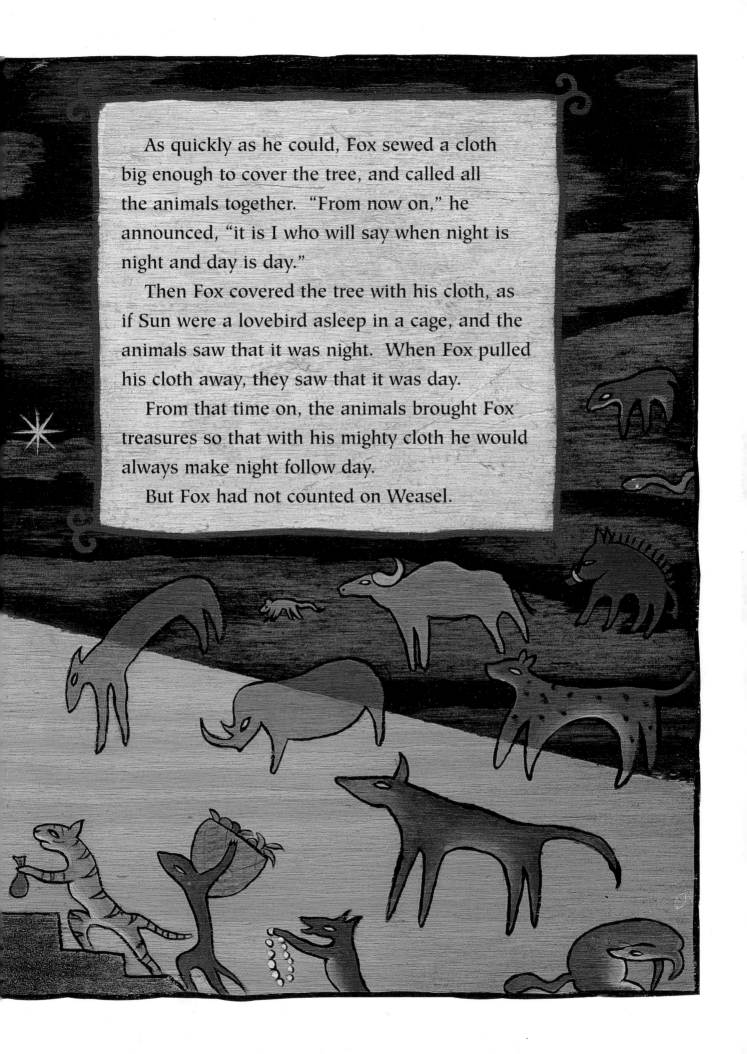

As quickly as he could, Fox sewed a cloth
big enough to cover the tree, and called all
the animals together. "From now on," he
announced, "it is I who will say when night is
night and day is day."

Then Fox covered the tree with his cloth, as
if Sun were a lovebird asleep in a cage, and the
animals saw that it was night. When Fox pulled
his cloth away, they saw that it was day.

From that time on, the animals brought Fox
treasures so that with his mighty cloth he would
always make night follow day.

But Fox had not counted on Weasel.

One day Weasel cut a hole as round as an eye in Fox's cloth, and hid the circle of cloth under a stone. That night the light shining through Weasel's hole made shadows come. They came in whispers, came on wind, through cracks in rocks and around black trees, watching.

"We run and hide," the animals said, "but still the shadows come."

"From now on," said Weasel, holding up her circle of cloth, "it is I who will say when night is night, because only I can make the shadows disappear." She held up her circle to the hole in Fox's cloth, and indeed the shadows disappeared.

But Weasel had not counted on Crow.

That night, when Weasel was asleep, Crow plucked the circle from the hole in Fox's cloth and announced to the animals, "From now on, it is I who will make the shadows disappear."

The animals were afraid and began to argue among themselves. Some sided with Fox, some with Weasel, and some with Crow. Soon bitter fights broke out, and it was not long before the animals brought war to the land.

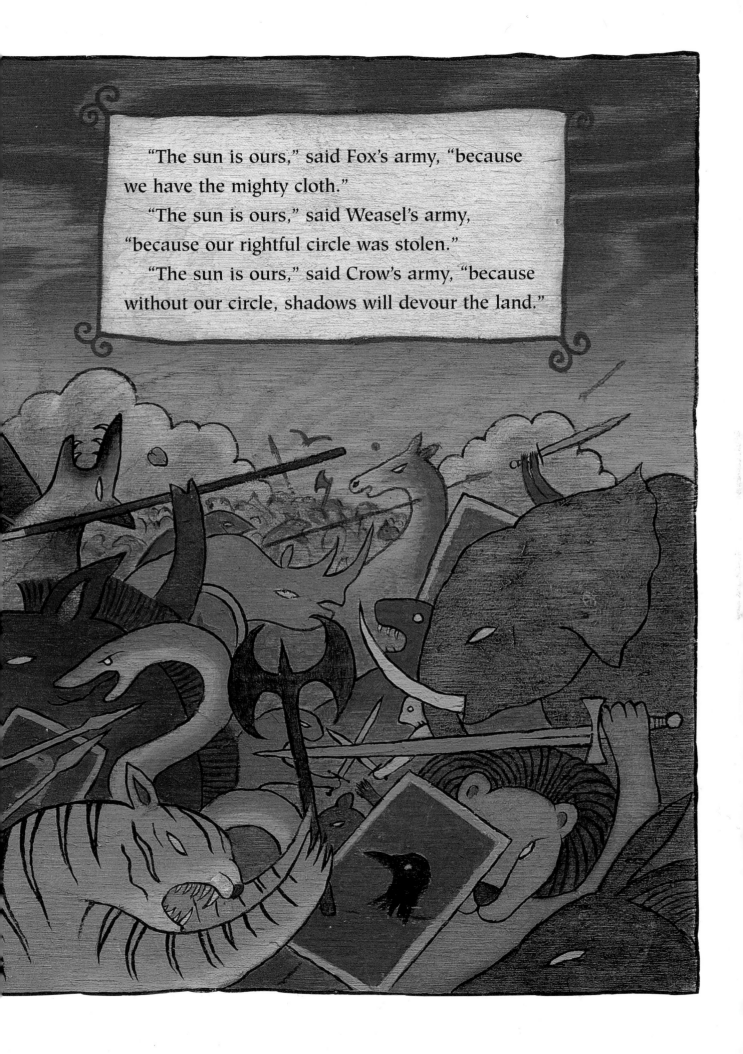

"The sun is ours," said Fox's army, "because we have the mighty cloth."

"The sun is ours," said Weasel's army, "because our rightful circle was stolen."

"The sun is ours," said Crow's army, "because without our circle, shadows will devour the land."

The animals fought long and hard. They burned the earth so rival armies would have no food. They cracked wings and bludgeoned fur, until they sat huddled together saying not a word, while shadows shivered in the land. As thin as ashes, gray as eyes, the shadows pressed their mouths against the wind, waiting.

It no longer mattered to the animals who was right and who was wrong, or whether it was night or day, or how the sun might be freed to hang once more like a jewel in the sky.

No one remembered what had happened to Fox's cloth, cut by Weasel and stolen by Crow, that now hung on the tree in shreds. No one remembered Sun, still caught like a beating heart in the hands of the tree.

Bear's Story

One night when all the animals lay sleeping,
Bear awakened just in time to see the moon slip
through a buttonhole of sky and fall to his feet
as if it were a ball no bigger than your hand.

"This cannot be," said Bear, rubbing his
eyes, but there Moon was, as round as a pearl
and white as milk, glistening.

"Aiiee," the animals said when they saw it.
"The moon is smaller than it seemed."
    Some thought Moon should be divided
among them, like coins in a purse, but Bear
shook his head. Of all the animals, he knew
the old stories best. "The moon is ours to tend
but not to own," he said.

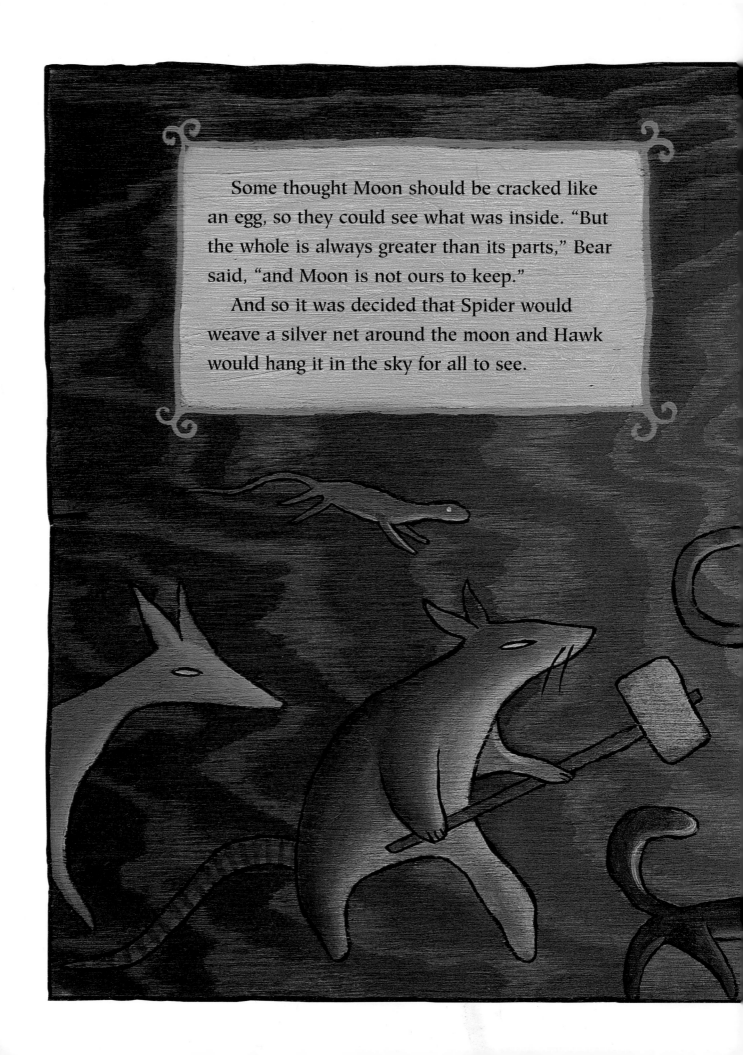

Some thought Moon should be cracked like an egg, so they could see what was inside. "But the whole is always greater than its parts," Bear said, "and Moon is not ours to keep."

And so it was decided that Spider would weave a silver net around the moon and Hawk would hang it in the sky for all to see.

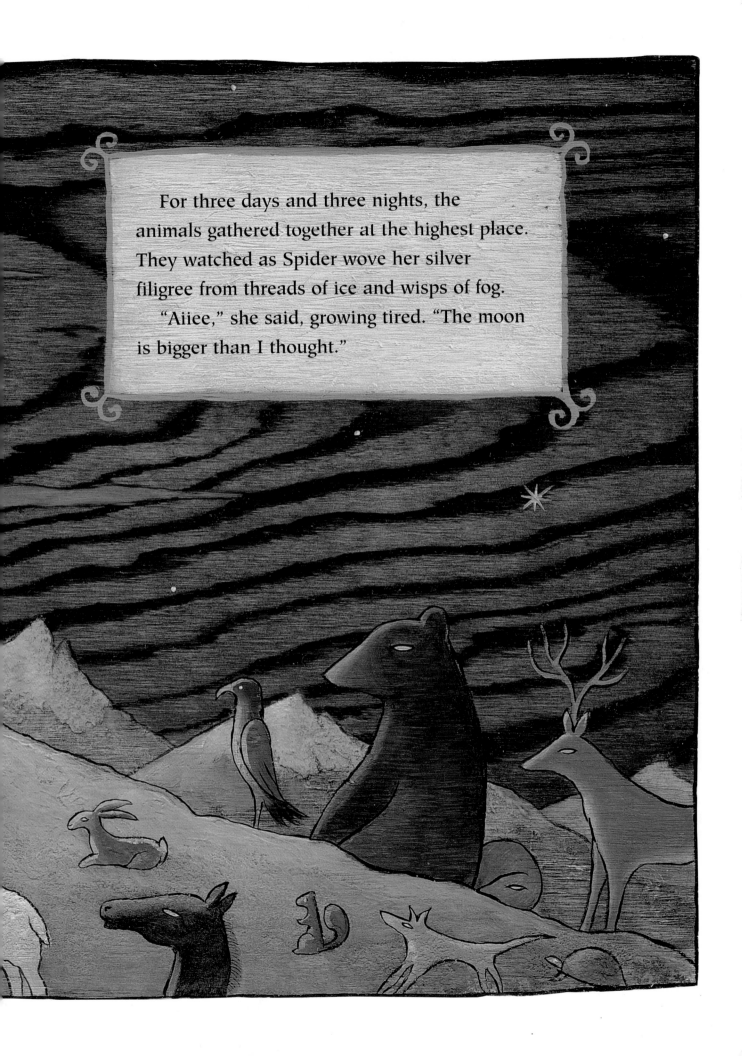

For three days and three nights, the animals gathered together at the highest place. They watched as Spider wove her silver filigree from threads of ice and wisps of fog.

"Aiiee," she said, growing tired. "The moon is bigger than I thought."

As Spider spun, she listened to Bear tell the stories. He told of Turtle who swam black waters again and again to bring back seeds so Summer could bake her bread. He told of Raccoon who every morning starched the clouds and hung them up to dry.

Finally, when Spider thought she could spin no more, the silver net was done.

The animals watched as Hawk took Moon's net in his strong beak. They saw him fly up higher than the tallest tree, higher than the nearest cloud, until he seemed no larger than a speck of earth in the sky.

"Aiiee," Hawk said, growing tired. "The sky is higher than I thought."

But Hawk remembered the stories that Bear had told–the story of how Rain and Wind braved Sun to make a hoop of many colors in the sky, the story of how Snake taught River to cut a path of singing through hardest rock.

Finally, when Hawk thought he could fly no farther, he reached Moon's home.

The animals below watched Hawk, his angel wings outspread, as he floated down like snow being rocked in a winter sky. They gave him food, they gave him drink, and he told them of his journey. From high above, he said, the earth's skin looked stitched together piece by piece. From higher still, it seemed a blue-green eye that watched the night.

"Remember well," he said to Bear. "You tell them so they won't forget."

From that time to this, Bear told the story of
when Moon tumbled from the sky–of how the
animals gathered together, how Spider wove a
silver net and Hawk flew high beyond the clouds.
And as the animals listened to Bear's story, they
could see Moon hang like an opal in an ebony
sky, shining.

The author is contributing part of the proceeds from this book to The Carter Center, a nonprofit, nonpartisan organization associated with Emory University in Atlanta, Georgia. Founded by former President Jimmy Carter and his wife, Rosalynn, the Center endeavors to resolve conflict, protect human rights, foster democracy and development, and fight poverty, hunger, and disease throughout the world.